For My Mother and Father

Clarion Books
a Houghton Mifflin Company imprint
215 Park Avenue South, New York, NY 10003
Lyrics of Roll Over from *Sally Go Round the Sun*
by Edith Fowler. Copyright © 1969 by McClelland and
Stewart Limited. Reprinted by permission of
Doubleday & Company, Inc.,
Illustrations copyright © 1981 by Merle Peek

For information about permission to reproduce
selections from this book write to Permissions,
Houghton Mifflin Company, 215 Park Avenue South, New York, NY 10003.
Printed in the USA

Library of Congress Cataloging in Publication Data
Peek, Merle.   Roll over.
Summary: Before going to sleep a little boy keeps
rolling over and as he does the 10 imaginary
animals that are crowded into the bed with him fall
out one after the other.
[1. Songs.   2. Counting.   3. Nursery rhymes]
I. Title.
PZ8.3.P2763Ro   398'8   80-16675
ISBN 0-395-29438-X   PA ISBN 0-395-58105-2

WOZ   20 19

ROLL OVER!

A Counting Song
Illustrated by MERLE PEEK

CLARION BOOKS

NEW YORK

10 in the bed
and the little one said:
   "ROLL OVER!
      ROLL OVER!"
They all rolled over
and one fell out.

9 in the bed
and the little one said:
"ROLL OVER!
ROLL OVER!"
They all rolled over
and one fell out.

8 in the bed
and the little one said:
"ROLL OVER!
ROLL OVER!"
They all rolled over
and one fell out.

7 in the bed
and the little one said:
  "ROLL OVER!
  ROLL OVER!"
They all rolled over
and one fell out.

6 in the bed
and the little one said:
  "ROLL OVER!
  ROLL OVER!"
They all rolled over
and one fell out.

5 in the bed
and the little one said:
   "ROLL OVER!
    ROLL OVER!"
They all rolled over
and one fell out.

4 in the bed
and the little one said:
"ROLL OVER!
ROLL OVER!"
They all rolled over
and one fell out.

3 in the bed
and the little one said:
"ROLL OVER!
ROLL OVER!"
They all rolled over
and one fell out.

2 in the bed
and the little one said:
   "ROLL OVER!
      ROLL OVER!"
They all rolled over
and one fell out.

1

in the bed
and the little one said:

"ALONE!
AT LAST!"

ROLL OVER

Ten in the bed and the little one said:
"Roll over! Roll over!"
They all rolled over and one fell out.

Nine in the bed and the little one said:
"Roll over! Roll over!"
They all rolled over and one fell out.

Eight in the bed. . .

Seven in the bed. . .

Six in the bed. . .

Five in the bed. . .

Four in the bed. . .

Three in the bed. . .

Two in the bed. . .

One in the bed and the little one said:
(*Spoken*) "Alone at last!"